French Quarter Tales

French Quarter Tales

Genaro Jesse Perez

FRENCH QUARTER TALES

iUniverse books may be ordered through booksellers or by contacting:

iUniverse
1663 Liberty Drive
Bloomington, IN 47403
www.iuniverse.com
844-349-9409

ISBN: 978-0-5954-2104-6 (sc)
ISBN: 978-1-4620-7755-7 (e)

Print information available on the last page.

iUniverse rev. date: 01/16/2021

"But now at intermission, with this shorthand scrawl on my knee, I don't feel exactly like talking like a critic, no comparative criticisms."

"The Pursuer"

Julio Cortázar

Contents

Couldn't Take My Eyes Off Of Her

February 5, 2004

Board of Pardons
Louisiana Parole Board
P.O. Box 94304
Baton Rouge, Louisiana 70804

TO WHOM IT MAY CONCERN

My attorneys have asked me to write a letter on my own behalf for the forthcoming hearing on my possible parole after serving thirty-seven years for killing a young woman, Ashley Robichaux, in New Orleans. Hopefully, the following narration will shed some light on my heinous behavior.

Several decades have passed since the tragic events I am about to narrate occurred, and yet, the incidents are still as vivid as if they had happened yesterday. But, in fact, they are like a dying sun swallowed by murky clouds. I was nineteen and had recently undergone the trauma of losing both of my parents in a plane crash. The cause, according to investigators, was wind sheer. As the plane was taking off from the New Orleans International Airport, one rainy morning, it crashed in the neighboring bayous. The irony was that it had been a chartered plane to Las Vegas where my parents were going for the weekend. There were no survivors. My father was a prominent attorney in the Crescent City and my mother was a professor of Comparative Literature at Tulane University. They had great expectations for me, either as an attorney, joining my father's firm, or becoming a professor at Tulane. I had failed to do well on the S.A.T exams, so that my only option was to attend Tulane as an English major thanks to my mother's position. Higher education bored me, so I attended the University to please my parents. After their death, I continued to attend, part-time, out of respect for their memory. I loved to read and I was writing poetry, so that attending classes and taking only the courses I cared for without seeking a degree, was my life for the moment. I considered myself an existential hero searching for a story. Hesse's novel, *Steppenwolf*, had become my favorite reading. The pronunciation of the German title **steppenvolf** sounded like music to my ears. But truly, my parents' death had driven me close to insanity. I wandered in a fog of sterile, toneless and flat days, frequently contemplating suicide and how to carry it out, moving in the shadows between rationality and insanity like a soldier warily stepping on a mine field. Suicide offered several possibilities: jumping into the Mississippi, using my father's gun, an overdose of sleeping pills, and many other possible actions depending on how dark the day was. During my most dismal moments, I would put my father's vintage Luger in my mouth while submerging myself in self-pity, envisioning the trajectory of the projectile and a crater erupting on the top of my head spewing blood and bones and brains. Father was a WWII veteran and had removed the gun from the body of a German officer who had committed suicide discharging it in his mouth. Father had joined the Army at seventeen at the tail end of the War and participated in the mopping-up of Berlin. He recalled vividly an event in that patch of his past when a machine-gun nest on the second floor of a building that had his squad immobilized. He managed to climb very close to it so as to throw a grenade that killed three German soldiers and, with the adrenalin flowing through his veins to the point he felt he could fly and do just about anything, he killed an additional one with his rifle as he charged into the room while at the same time receiving a light wound on his upper arm. As he went through the door, a Captain in the German army was putting the gun into his mouth and firing. My father was decorated with a Silver Star for gallantry in action and received a Purple Heart for the wound. He loved to retell the anecdote, indulging in the gory details of the crater on the top of the German's head and the blood and bones covering it. I could almost taste the metal and the oil of the barrel, for my father had spent many hours cleaning and oiling it after his forays into the swamps shooting at everything that moved. The barrel of the gun was like a pacifier evoking the early years in my life when sucking a rubber nipple lulled me to sleep during those solitary nights with my parents away on their long trips, leaving me alone with my black nanny. My only companion then was a calico cat that spent most of her time in my bedroom, sleeping at my feet. Evidently my psyche was too fragile to stand the lost of loved ones. I was ten years old the first time I became aware of my flaw—if that is the proper term. My calico cat, Calita, at the age of eight, was found dead in our back yard. It was the first time I confronted the death of a loved one. My severe depression required spending over a year with an analyst. I remained under Dr. Thompson's care until at last managing to forget about Calita and her presence in my bedroom from my second birthday onward. Being unwilling to begin visiting a psychiatrist again, I managed to find three physicians who provided me with a substantial amount of bennies and downers to keep me up when desirable, and able to sleep when sufficiently tired. Finding a steady supplier of marihuana increased my chemical defenses against depression and suicide. Most of these years are shrouded in mist and my recollection of Ashley is the only vivid memory of that period.

Thanks to my medical history of psychological trauma and the help of my father's firm, a "4F" classification for military service enabled me to avoid the Viet Nam War. While many friends and acquaintance who graduated or dropped out of college were drafted, mine was a life of leisure without concerning myself with a far-away war.

I sold my parents' house in the Garden District and bought a townhouse on St. Phillip, in the French Quarter. My inheritance of four million dollars from my parents resulted from their life insurance, assets for survivors from the law firm, several investments my father had, and real estate property in Kenner. All of those assets were liquidated and converted to a combination of bonds, as suggested by the law firm's accountant, making me a man of property and leisure thanks to the monthly income these investments provided. Despite drifting through life without having to work, without financial concerns, I was as unhappy as a drunk living on Skid Row.

Since literature came easy for me—perhaps my mother's influence and genes—I had been concentrating on it and ignoring the usual requirements for a degree. Mother had had a great influence on my love for literature. From my earliest memories, I was in her arms, nursing from her breast as she read from a series of books. She also wrote a great deal, publishing literary criticism in many journals, as well as books in prestigious university presses. I cherished the moments before going to bed when she described to me the horrors she witnessed and the perils she went through before arriving in the U.S. at the age of eight. At the moment of her untimely demise, my poor mother had been recording her experiences in her memoirs. Her life had been extraordinary and eventful: escaping the Holocaust, night rides, hiding in ruins and under bridges.... All those things were now lost like weeping willow leaves crushed by a storm or tears evaporated in a rain of fire. She took a thick notebook with a leather cover everywhere as her Germanic upbringing prodded her to write all those memories, that were like snapshots in her mind, every available moment. Her remembrances will not be shared with anyone since the only copy was burned in the crash.

My parents named me for my father and grandfather. Actually, I was the fourth in the line of Claude Courbets beginning in the middle of the Nineteenth Century with my great-grandfather, a river-boat captain on the Mississippi river. I told my friends and acquaintances that my name was Harry, since I really did not care for my first name and mother had given me as middle name her father's, Heinrich.

Having accumulated numerous courses in English with excellent grades convinced the Chair of the English Department to allow me to take two graduate seminars. One was on Twentieth Century British Poets and the other on James Joyce, where I met Ashley, a doctoral student finishing her course work. In my journals and dreams she was Hermina, the beautiful woman in *Steppenwolf.*

Following these evening classes, I would go home, change into some old jeans, a t-shirt and some old Mexican sandals with soles made from automobile tires. After a frugal meal, reading a few pages from a book or magazine and ingesting a couple of bennies and smoking a joint, I would arrive at the **Seven Seas** around eleven. I carried with me a mochila, a Mexican peasant bag, where I kept the pistol, a small note-book where I wrote poetry plus any impressions worth writing and/or remembering, my wallet and a couple of bennies, in case I came down too soon. The **Seas** was located on Saint Phillip about two blocks from my house. I did not have a car and my trips to Tulane on class days took 40–45 minutes by street car each way. Given the difficulties of parking in the Quarter, I had sold our three cars and did not miss my Mustang. When one lives in the Quarter one tends to remain there without going too far out of it. The Quarter becomes a microcosm favoring suspension of ethical values and the typical mores: commonplace laws are discontinued in favor of a bohemian life-style and freedom not found elsewhere. To live in the Quarter meant living in a perpetual moral holiday where time disappeared and all the days were Saturdays.

The **Seven Seas** was a bar frequented by the locals after 11:00 p.m. Before eleven, it was usually filled with tourists and teenagers. During these years, the legal drinking age in New Orleans was eighteen and the **Seas** filled with teeny-boppers whose parents expected them home by midnight. The bar had been once upon a time a large Eighteenth Century residence. Robbed of its walls, it was now one large single room that extended 50 feet from North to South and 30 feet from East to West. At the western part of the room was a large bar with stools covering one fourth of the room and a wall mirror with shelves that held a myriad of bottles of liquor. The entrance to the bar was located at the southern part on the side of the bar so that all the newcomers passed by the bar first, buying their drinks as they entered, and then moved on to the eastern part of the room to the tables and booths. The only light in this area was provided by three pseudo-Tiffany lamps hanging over three chess tables, in the center of the room, where many customers played chess practically twenty-four hours daily since the bar never closed. Inasmuch as the bar had only two small fluorescent lights close to the ceiling where the mirror ended, the entire room remained in perpetual duskiness, a permissive twilight, except in the early morning when the janitors cleaned the floors and bathrooms of the vomit, papers, gum, rubbers, needles, cigarette butts and other trash left by the customers. Leaning against and midway of the eastern wall, a jukebox endlessly played popular songs. I frequently fed it quarters and played "I can't keep my eyes off of you," the Frankie Vallie hit of the previous year. I would then look at her from my throne, her beautiful face now faded by time like a photograph exposed to the sun, and smiled whenever her steely blue eyes strayed my way, and I whispered along with the song "I love you baby…."

On the Northwest side of the room, a corridor led to the restrooms and the patio, where those who did not know any better tried to smoke weed and were frequently busted by narcs that frequented the place. On the edge of the corridor stood my throne, a broken, old ping-ball machine that I used as a perch. Since my father had known the owner of "The Seas" very well, I was the only person allowed to sit on the tall side of the ping-ball machine, which offered a wonderful vista of the entire room and, for the most part, the shadows of the people in it. Most importantly, I could see her face always sitting at the same place in the southwest part of the bar. When I played the song, sometimes our eyes would meet as the juke box played "you are too good to be true," and sometimes she would smile back, a Mona Lisa type of smile where the eyes, her clear blue eyes, her sparkling blue eyes that reflected the neon signs of beers and liquors framing and peppering the large rectangular mirror of the bar, were doing the smiling. "I wanna hold you so much." Weeks and then months passed before I finally developed the courage to speak to her. Although we were in the same seminar, nothing favored interaction between the two of us until one night she was leaving rather late, apparently unable to walk straight, and I offered to walk her home. I took her to her apartment two blocks beyond my town house and, to my surprise, after inviting me to prepare her and myself some coffee, she returned from the bathroom totally nude. I must explain at this point that I have difficulty interacting with women. The only woman I had known carnally at this point was a prostitute. When I was fourteen, my father felt I was too close to my mother and that my behavior was feminized, and, therefore, he considered it his duty to make sure I did not become a homosexual. He took me to a very private and exclusive bordello in Jefferson Parish where a young woman introduced me to sex. The entire episode embarrassed me to the point where I had kept myself from having sex since then. As a result of my ignorance, the experience with Hermina was a disaster. I ejaculated prematurely and she was very annoyed. But she was heaven to touch! As my fingers moved about her body, her alabaster skin, her red hair, a Pre-Raphaelite model, the rosettas crowning her breasts and her erect red nipples gorged with blood were very arousing and my self-control failed. Thereafter she did not speak to me and she never looked in my direction at "The Seas." I was devastated; even though she was almost a decade older than I, I wrote to her proposing matrimony: I revealed how much money I had and swore to make her the happiest woman in the world. She did not reply to my letters and then one night, at the Seas, a gorilla warned me to stay away from her if I wanted to stay healthy. At this point my stalking of Hermina began. I contacted the make-up artist of the Pretenders Little Theater on Dumaine and Saint Ann who sold me several wigs and showed me how to change my appearance without ever asking me compromising questions. Using several different costumes, I followed her practically everywhere she went in the Quarter. Until one evening, as I watched, behind a car, across the street from her apartment, I saw her kissing another woman. They stopped kissing and looked in my direction and started to laugh. A cloud entered my brain and I only remember taking the gun from the bag, crossing the street and shooting both of them. I inserted the gun in my mouth and pulled the trigger, but it jammed. Suddenly, I felt a blow on my face and fainted. When I awoke, I was handcuffed and traveling in a police car. The trial was swift and thanks to my age and my state of mind, the judge was merciful and did not sentence me to death. I thank God I am alive. I hereby throw myself on the mercy of the Board and request that I be paroled.

Thank you very much for your kind attention to this matter. I look forward to hearing from you.

Very truly yours,

Claude H. Courbets

DREAMDEMONS

It all began during his chemo treatments for breast cancer. "It was highly unusual," people said, especially the doctors who had repeatedly told him that the discharge from the left nipple was harmless and not to forget that *men did not get breast cancer*. Rage at their ignorance surged within Gerard Pierre Tourveil, a volcano about to explode, when the oncologist explained that roughly 15% of breast cancers occur in men, leaving him resentful and depressed. The nights following the nine-to-five days at the medical school, having the drug pumped into Gerard Pierre's circulatory system through the "port" in his chest, were more conducive to hallucinated dreams. It was the process for taming the beast, as he called the cancer in his body. The nightmares would subside after three to four days until the next weekly dose of medicine that would hopefully kill all the cancer cells that had invaded his body, no matter where they were hidden. Those two or three nights, particularly the first one, were filled with horror. In a twilight half-sleep, Gerard witnessed the most horrendous decapitations, amputations of limbs and "deglovings," and heard bone-chilling shrieks. Gerard Pierre Tourveil wanted to scream himself, put an end to the slice-and-dice images and the aural/oral accompaniment, but could not. Gerard was all alone in the house except for his two cats who would lie on his chest, helping him deal with the nightmares. Gerard Pierre's wife had absconded a year earlier with one of her graduate students and was now teaching on the East coast, at another university. Gerard was an Instructor in English at the University of New Orleans without tenure or hope of ever finishing his doctoral degree from Tulane. They had kept him on, for about ten years now, teaching three-fourths of the time with one course in the summer, which allowed him to rent a small efficiency in the Quarter. With his wife's income, the economic situation had been ideal, but now Gerard Pierre Tourveil could not work and with the cancer … he worried about his future. Gerard hoped to be cured and that the hallucinations would stop once the effects of the chemo wore away, leaving his body cancer-free. Unfortunately, his dreamed-of outcome did not come to pass. Instead, the hallucinations became more eidetic and he found himself taking part in sanguinary orgies. Gerard would wake up frequently with blood stains on his pajamas, feeling he had walked the darkened halls of Hell: it was a terror that could not be told; an unspeakable horror. He saw the three ugly heads of Cerberus facing him, his dragon-jaws opened wide, his lips drawn back in a grin of fangs. And his body had changed so much: he had gained over thirty pounds thanks to the marihuana that enhanced his appetite and maintained the nausea and vomiting at a minimum. All his curly black hair, inherited from his Acadian ancestors, was gone. Most of it fell out in the shower, like leaves from the trees in winter, which he cleaned slowly as he thought about his mortality, life and death. The rest of the hair, that appeared like tiny islands on his body, he shaved. Even his copious pubic hair was gone. Frequently, as Gerard stood in front of the bathroom's full-length mirror, his hairless genitalia reminded him of the first time he examined his nakedness in front of a mirror: he was about six and the mirror in his grandfather's Garden District home, was high above the basin, so he climbed upon the basin to examine his genitals. Everything was so complicated now, and by contrast, how happy and wonderful those childhood years with the whole family in the Tourveil mansion had been. As the nightmares became progressively gorier, their reality was accentuated by his bloody pajamas and the cuts, bites and bruises on his body. Even worse were the various instruments of torture and knives of different shapes and dimensions that he kept finding, caked with layers of blood and bits of epidermis. He had no one to turn to, his sanity was suspect and Gerard Pierre Tourveil was at a loss, totally confused as to what he should do. Gerard decided to sleep as little as possible, living on coffee and bennies to restrain the nightmares, which seemed to work at first, but soon made them more intense until the nightmare metamorphosed into reality: he found himself on a strange bed astride a woman's bloody corpse, wielding a butcher knife. Gerard Pierre Tourveil was convicted of serial killing, having drawn and quartered seven women, all somehow eerily resembling his wife.

BLACK KNIGHT

He was born with his left thumb missing and it constituted a source of a great pain throughout his twenty-one years. First in grammar school and High School, and then in college, he was treated as a freak. He dreamed of becoming a physician as had his grandfather, rather than a famous (or infamous) trial attorney like his father. His family had roots that went far back into Louisiana's history. He was a St. Clair and, notwithstanding the fact that his branch of the family had dropped to lower-middle-class status because of his father's incompetence and asinine investments, he continued to be very proud of his family name. Pierre August St. Clair was named after his grandfather and cared little for his father, Roy. Pierre's mother died before he was ten and by that time the family fortune had begun to evaporate. Fortunately, his standing as a "legacy" and the fact that his grandfather had endowed several professorships at Tulane University, assured his access to college education. While not bright, Pierre was tenacious and liked to read and, as a result, his grades at Jesuit High were very good. He entered Tulane without the typical problems students encounter in the first years of college. Pierre August moved out of his father's home to reside in the New Orleans French Quarter where he could submerge himself in a bohemian atmosphere while studying without his father's intolerable presence.

For three years Pierre took pre-med requirements receiving A's in most of his classes so that he was convinced that Medical Schools would be competing to have him attend their program. To his dismay, the Chair of the Department of Zoology, Professor John Kent, on whose recommendation he was counting to enter Medical School, informed him that Pierre's handicap was an insurmountable stumbling block and that he could not write a letter on his behalf. Pierre was devastated: a whirlpool of emotions overwhelmed him, nauseating him so that he ran out of Professor Kent's office immediately to vomit in the nearest men's room. Pierre associated the spurt of vomit with the smell of violets that frequently exudes from a decomposing body and it left a vile taste in his mouth. The white commode, stained with a brownish film, the remains of the jambalaya and black beans he had two hours earlier for lunch, overshadowed his consciousness and nightmares in the coming days.

That incident changed Pierre's life and thereafter he turned to literature and philosophy to escape what he bitterly considered one of life's many injustices. Since his apartment in the Quarter was only a block from "The Seven Seas," a bar frequented by residents and students from Tulane and U.N.O., he became a habitual customer. The building where the bar was located had large windows with iron grille-work, and high ceilings, that kept the buildings cool and airy in the summers before air-conditioning was invented. A sign several feet long protruded from the facade of the white-washed wall, a replica of a pirate's ship carved out of cherry wood with the name "The Seven Seas" in burnt green on the gunwales, above two tiny rows of cannons. A bowsprit in the shape of a bare-chested maiden extended forward from the stem. Inside, benches, stools, tables, lamps, life preservers, and other assorted oddities were scattered throughout, underscoring the nautical motif. Four tables offered facilities for playing chess. From the four hand-sawed wooden ceiling beams, bleached by time, hung four small light bulbs dressed with multicolored paper shades and red fringes—the pseudo-Tiffany type shade sold in most of the Quarter's tourist traps. The smallness of the bulbs immersed the room in perpetual twilight that hung over the four chess tables directly beneath the Tiffany-shaded light bulbs.

Pierre spent most nights playing chess at the "Seas," a game he had played with his grandfather since he was seven, experience placing him near a master's level. By defeating almost everyone that challenged him, he sublimated the anger and hate he now felt for humankind. Pierre August St. Clair had decreed that ethics and morality were irrelevant and the laws of society likewise.

Before his traumatic conversation with Professor Kent, Pierre was relatively self-conscious about his handicap; afterward, he embarked upon an obsessive sojourn to hide his missing extremity. He had a black glove made with a false thumb and wore the glove at all times, while keeping the hand in his pocket whenever possible. While playing chess, however, Pierre kept that hand visible and, as a result, he became known at the "Seas" as "Black Knight." Furthermore, as part of a strategy to devastate those who played him, Pierre always chose the black pieces.

Yet another vagary singled Pierre out from most of the other freaks that frequented the "Seas": he played on the jukebox the theme from "Elvira Madigan," a movie he had seen and liked. The music was actually Mozart's Concert No. 21 for piano and, because it had been the most popular record that year, the melody managed to carve a niche in the jukebox among the Stones, the Beatles, Bob Dylan and Jimmy Hendrix. Pierre would usually put the coin in the machine and mark D7 before starting a game and the record somehow was played by the busy jukebox of the "Seas" within the ten to fifteen minutes that his challengers generally managed to survive.

One Friday, very close to midnight, Pierre saw her for the first time. Most of the patrons had already fallen under the spell of alcohol or the drug of their choice (the Seas was a good place to score grass, bennies, and even smack), and they were no longer interested in playing chess. Pierre busily scribbled impressions about the previous game in a note book he toted with him and where he also wrote poems when the inspiration struck him. As Pierre August wrote, he heard Mozart's concert beginning to play and, shortly thereafter, one of the most beautiful women he had ever seen sat down in front of him and asked for a game. She was rather androgynous, with her red hair cut very short, a la Mia Farrow. Her eyes were intensely blue and, he thought, the stereotypical bedroom eyes he had read and heard so much about. Pierre had little experience with women—he had only known two. The apparition, as he began to think of her, had rosy flesh that glowed even under the dim cone of light that showered the chess table. Pierre recalled the pre-Raphaelite beauties he had studied in his art history class. She used very little make-up and was wearing a western blouse, jeans and a denim vest. The item of clothing that surprised Pierre the most was the biker boots with small chains strapped around them. He assumed immediately that she was a Lesbian, part of the gay community residing in the Quarter. They played, and for the first time in countless games, he lost.

She (to be called by any name since she told Pierre to select one), Elvira or Elvie, Pierre's choice, would appear at the Seas, every other week on average, playing a game or two with him, before disappearing in the Quarter's enchanted nights. Elvira's outfits were different, but the motif and clothing were the same: pants, blouse, vest and the biker boots. One Saturday evening she informed Pierre Augustus that she had concluded that the reason he could not defeat her was a lack of motivation and that if he won that night, he could take her to his place and do with her whatever he wished. Pierre, a sexually inexperienced young man to whom women were a conundrum still to be deciphered, concluded she was mocking him but tried to play as well as he could and he won. One can always wonder if she allowed him to win or if he simply played a better game that night but, in any event, he was convinced she was being facetious. When Elvira said to him, I am yours tonight, he finally realized he was about to make love to his White Goddess.

Elvie, Pierre discovered, knew a great deal about sex and those positions that intensified not only her orgasms, but also Pierre's, and he quickly became an adept apprentice. Elvie's sexual philosophy was that as long as both partners enjoyed whatever they were doing, anything was acceptable. Elvie preferred either the one thousand cranes position or to be penetrated in the anus. Pierre discovered two things about himself as a result of his affair with Elvie: he loved sex and he was very well endowed.

The affair went on for months. Since she asked for a key to his apartment and exacted the promise that he would never follow her nor try to probe her identity, he never knew when he would see her next: she would appear in the middle of night when he was already in bed, or in the mornings as he was preparing to go to school, but never again at the Seas. As a result, while at home, Pierre spent his time wondering when he would see her again. Sometimes she would not appear for two weeks, provoking miserable, dark days of despair during which Pierre concluded she had found someone else. But then, there she was again, magically appearing before his bed in the middle of the night, while at a distance, one could hear someone singing the blues. Then Pierre was glad he was not blue anymore.

Pierre August's existence was now divided into before Elvie and after Elvie. Before her, Pierre's life was meaningless—a bus ride taking him nowhere, merely existing; a state of inaction and, even behind every undertaking, every class he attended, every shower he took in the mornings, there was nothing until there was Elvie. With Elvie he felt complete and life held meaning beyond his most florid dreams, despite Professor Kent's refusal to write a letter of recommendation for Medical School.

But the moment he most feared arrived before he was aware of it. Two months, and then three passed and Elvie did not visit him. In Pierre's recurring nightmares she was with another man walking down the Quarter's streets and, as he approached them, calling her name, she disappeared. Pierre would awake bathed in his own perspiration still calling Elvie in his shadowy, gloomy room. And yet, desperately hoping to see her again, Pierre August returned to the Seas and played chess and walked down the Quarter streets looking at every female that resembled Elvira. But the weight of Giant Despair was crushing him and despair was inside him and everywhere around him. Immersed in the dark fog of melancholy with no one to rescue him, his chess playing was no longer outstanding so he now had to wait in line to play. He no longer attended his classes and feared his nightmares so much that he slept very little.

One Sunday morning, as he perused *The Times-Picayune* he had bought, standing on the corner of Saint Peter and Rue Royal, as the morning mist fanned about the Quarter like lost tourists, and covered the rooftops like a white sheet straddling old furniture, he saw Elvie's photograph on the front page. The story indicated she was from a prominent New Orleans family; a former Queen of the Krew of Rex, with two young girls and married to a prominent attorney. Her husband had shot her and her lover upon finding them in a very intimate position. The story continued on page two and, as he turned the page, standing petrified on the corner of Rue Royal and Saint Peter, he was astounded to see his own photograph reproduced from his Tulane student identification. Upon reading the lines identifying him as the lover killed by the jealous husband, he dropped the paper as if it were on fire. A whirling Quarter wind playfully swept up the pages of newsprint and carried them a short distance as Pierre August disappeared, leaving no trace, as if he had not been there at all.

Shrines

Raymond Ernest Robichaux, whose few acquaintances called him Ray, felt very unhappy with his life. Raymond Ernest found himself counting the days until his two-week vacation. Raymond had been a pre-med major in college, graduating with a B.S. in Chemistry from the University of New Orleans and had applied to several medical schools without success.

Desperate and adrift for months, Raymond attended a jobs fair and while visiting one of the many kiosks with large signs and filled with brochures touting the corporation's accomplishments and wonderful benefits available to the employees, he obtained information on a seemingly exciting pharmaceutical company. Raymond Ernest Robichaux applied for a position as a pharmaceutical rep for a well known-international conglomerate and accepted immediately when they offered him the post. He had to drive from New Orleans's French Quarter, where he rented an efficiency, to three states: East Texas from Dallas to Houston, and the entire states of Louisiana and Mississippi. Ray drove a 1998 Ford Taurus which consumed very little gasoline and allowed him to save on his travel stipend. He stayed in cheap motels, saving the difference for himself. Most such motels had a faintly musty smell that reminded Ray of the odor permeating the oncologists' offices he so frequently visited. The musty smell was perhaps from the baseboards' dampness that never went away, eventually becoming part of the environs. Raymond decided to save as much as possible and resign in a few years.

Ray Ernest did not care much for his job which entailed visiting dozens of oncologists' offices, sometimes six days per week. While waiting to promote his wares, he had to witness a parade of unhealthy bodies that remained with him no matter how much he tried to erase them from his memory: Ray could not get the myriad of wretched figures out of his head. Pale, moon-faced women with no hair and bulging eyes like deers' frozen in the headlights; skeletal men with skin so yellow one could see the blood vessels beneath, like the road maps Raymond had to consult before memorizing his route that took him to back roads and small towns. In some instances, the coughing and the handkerchiefs stained with blood turned his stomach so violently that Ray couldn't eat even hours after witnessing such incidents.

Ray was not a happy man. His mother, Donna, an Irish woman, had left his father, Ernest, and returned to Ireland when he was barely ten. Ernest drank himself to death while listening to unhappy ballads from the fifties. All those songs lamenting how the lover had gone away inundated their apartment during Ray's teen years. By the time Ray was 18, his father had died from a heart attack and cirrhosis of the liver.

Ray himself was abandoned by the love of his life, Sandy, while they were still in college. Sandy and Ray had been high-school sweethearts notwithstanding their belonging to different social classes. She was from an old Louisiana family, the Landries, members of the Krew of Comus since the nineteenth century, and her father and mother had been King and Queen during Mardi Gras. Sandy had attended Sacred Heart School, a private nuns' school for girls. Ray's ancestors were Acadian and dirt-poor and, because his father had worked as janitor for Jesuit High and Ray was very studious and bright, he managed to obtain a scholarship at Jesuit. The Catholic girls' and boys' schools' Friday dances during the school year provided the occasion when Ray and Sandy met. He fell madly in love with her but never felt sure how much she loved him. While Sandy was a pre-med student at Tulane, Ray was studying pre-med at the University of New Orleans, but she was accepted by a Medical School on the East Coast, precipitating the break-up of their relationship. Ray, bitter and obsessed with the notion that perhaps Sandy was as fast as the Beamer her family gave her upon acceptance into medical school, worried that he had been blinded by his love or his hope that she would become his wife, not realizing how egotistical she truly was.

Delving into the past, he remembered weekends when Sandy had left campus to see her parents at their cabin in Bay Saint Louis, and he had been unable to contact her. There were also the parties at her sorority when she had danced with other men, much to Raymond's displeasure. Ray's childhood memories, which sometimes intruded into his consciousness like unwanted house guests, were his father's drinking and unhappy love ballads drifting from a record player. Since his mother's name was Donna, his father had worn-out several copies of the Ritchie Valens song by that name. Sometimes the words would come into his brain and without realizing it he would be murmuring: *I had a girl, Donna was her name, since she left me, I've never been the same.* Ray had inherited his father record collection and transferred it to tapes. Masochistically, he now took them on his long trips, replaying those same unhappy love songs: Tommy Edward's "It's all in the game," The Fleetwood's "Mr. Blue," Roy Orbison's "Only the Lonely," Johnnie Ray's "I'll never fall in love again" and "Cry."

After several months as a pharmaceutical rep, Raymond Ernest Robichaux began experiencing a recurrent dream endowed with the quality of vivid recall when he awoke, staring at the faces of patients from the doctors' offices. But now, they were flagitious, menacing and grotesque, as though transposed from horror movies. Their eyes were fierce and bloodshot with flecks of blood and foam covering their lips. Ray didn't actually begin to worry about his sanity until the heinous shapes began appearing along the road. Coincidentally, the phantom shapes appeared in certain spots noticed during previous trips, which he had mentally termed "shrines," places where a fatal accident had occurred and friends and relatives of the victims placed crosses, flowers, photos, or even toys, if a child had perished. These shrines were far and few between, but the stark apparitions were disconcerting enough to cause Ray to consider visiting a psychiatrist. He decided to drive more often during the daylight hours in the event his eyes and the effects of darkness were causing the hallucinations. To his dismay, the figures began appearing during the daylight hours as well. The ghosts, for he had concluded they were not of this world, simply stood there, apparently looking at him. When Ray saw them at night, the headlights added a dimension missing during the day when they seemed translucent. Frequently, trauma to the head and face had bloodied the features of the ghosts, and their limbs suggested those of dolls that children had cruelly deformed. Raymond Ernest Robichaux realized he must confront these demons, and so, he stopped the car when he next spotted the figures and rushed to the site on foot often risking being killed by automobiles on the highway, the occupants of which often blew their horns and shouted profanities. To Ray's dismay, the ghosts had disappeared once he reached the particular shrine. After such experiences, upon returning to his car, Ray's body trembled as if in a freezer unclad or overcome with fever, and his stomach contracted with nausea, not so much from fear as dread of the unknown. Ray fought the desire to remain, waiting for the apparitions' return; feelings beyond his control or understanding kept him there, not allowing him to leave or to recover.

Several phantasmal incidents later, he began to accompany his driving by low continuous humming, sometimes singing along with the taped songs, mainly to keep himself from thinking about the apparitions. Raymond was morose every day, suddenly weary and sullen, gradually drowning himself in despair with no idea what to do about it. A tsunami of emotions overwhelmed him.

One night in the early fall, after a long rainy day, during his return from Texas to New Orleans, while driving somewhere between Lafayette and Baton Rouge, as he passed Grosse Tete and Whiskey Bay, when the fog rose from the bayous and filaments of angel-spittle—or still more relevant—of devil-spit were covering the highway, another ghostly figure materialized on the wide shoulder of I–10. He had been listening to Johnnie Ray's "Cry" and as he sang along "when your sweetheart sends a letter of goodbye …" his eyes moistened and blurred like his vision of the pavement, the trees and the brush outside, reliving the letter from Sandy terminating their relationship. The figure on the shoulder of the road looked so familiar that he stopped and ran back into the cold evening drizzle, drawn irresistibly to the apparition. As Raymond reached the place something extraordinary happened: this time the figure did not vanish. Examining it closely, he discovered, to his stupor, that it looked very much like himself covered with blood, the skin white as chalk and the vitreous eyes wide open. Panic-stricken, he fainted, awakening in an ambulance with the siren echoing the pain tearing through his head and most of his body.

I pulled Ray's crushed, bloody body from the wrecked Taurus. He barely had time to speak and recount his experience before he died as we arrived at Baton Rouge General where I work. Ray gave me his pocket diary, asking that I tell his unlikely story. The diary provided additional information Ray had not had time to reveal. Despite the story's implausibility, I feel the fact that it was Raymond's last request obligates me to repeat it.

PATIENT # H35927S99
AKA “MISTER LUCKY”

In my twenty-plus years of practicing psychiatry, the patient known as "Mister Lucky" represents a significant case study of a graduated march into insanity. Since the patient kept a notebook giving an account of his daily encounters with the slot machine, an authoritative basis exists that allows one to summarize his perspective on life and the world around him. Thus we may use his own words, not only written, but also the taped conversations held throughout his confinement at Biloxi General before his departure and unfortunate demise. Jargon has been eliminated because the publishers feel that this monograph, the first in a projected collection of case studies, should interest the general public who would better appreciate it if most technical terms are omitted.

The enchanting power of his favorite machine is described by Mister Lucky in his notebooks as spiritual experiences, epiphanies, mystical episodes: as he stared at the hypnotic wheels of the slot-machine, those spinning little squares illustrating brave and evil, real and unreal, cartoonish figures, and the flashing kaleidoscope of fluctuating, metamorphosing, multi-colored lights, listening hypnotized by the cornucopia of variegated sounds spewed out by strategically-placed speakers, his pulse began to gallop and adrenaline rushed through his veins (like a Formula One racer doing his last lap), and the high became a mystical occurrence where he could virtually reach out and touch God and nearly understand His grand design, and the participation of chance, so clear and yet so subtle, just as inconceivable as his winning so frequently in that same penny machine he played everyday, that gave him enough mini-jackpots to sustain himself with very little in Biloxi. But later, when his fortune changed (he claimed the machine was doctored to keep him from winning), his depths of depression were unmeasurable; he described the low as falling into a bottomless pit. During those instances shortly before he was committed, he would get up and walk away from the machine in what he termed an out-of-body experience where he saw himself ambling in a fog into which all the players in the Casino disappeared, while his stomach, and his head too, fluttered like a demented whirling-dervish dancer.

Mr. Lucky had dropped out of Mississippi State University halfway through his sophomore year. Since he read very slowly, was dyslexic and the sciences did not appeal to him, he found no appropriate calling among the many majors the University had to offer. Mister Lucky did not expect much from life. A wife and children were something beyond his concerns at the age of twenty, so he found employment as a salesperson in a shoe department at Biloxi's mall. In the evenings he would go to Beau Rivage and spend a couple of hours playing the slot machines. This routine he followed over some three years until the fated day when the machine of his life arrived.

She was among a set of four machines that were installed in a very prominent area of the Casino (adjacent to the buffet), one April afternoon as Lucky played nearby. Two of the machines were called Mr. Lucky and the other two were Ms. Lucky. The Mr. Lucky machines had female voices that resembled Marilyn Monroe's, whereas the Ms. Lucky machines featured a male voice reminiscent of Humphrey Bogart. As a result, most men, including the patient in question, played Mr. Lucky, while most women engaged Ms. Lucky. The voices in question cooed with bedroom nuances, whenever the player won over two-thousand coins, "you are so lucky, Mr. Lucky," or, in the case of the other two machines, "you are so lucky, Ms. Lucky." The patient began playing one of the Mr. Lucky machines and found himself repeatedly winning small sums. Every time he won, Marilyn's voice praised him and informed him he was a very lucky man, while simultaneously playing the theme song of a popular television program with the same name as the machine. When he lost, which was seldom, her silence, according to the patient, was both painful and bewildering.

Mister Lucky's good fortune with the machine evolved over three years during which time he could spend up to twelve hours with the machine (usually from 9:00 p.m. to 9:00 a.m.) and be ahead by two hundred dollars. He moved into the hotel and between winnings and comps, he slept, ate and drank at the Beau Rivage. He won at least two mini-jackpots per week in the amounts of $500.00 and $800.00. Those amounts were consumed briskly by the room at the hotel and his meals at expensive restaurants. The winning of the jackpot was announced by the machine with Marilyn's voice singing engagingly with her bedroom voice, the melody of a song written expressly for the machine:

OOO! You're soo Lucky
Mister Lucky
I want to share my life with you
For I want to be lucky too
Come, come to me now my lucky love
and tell me, tell me
you love me true!

All the machine lights would blink, a deafening cacophony would erupt, and then, a few minutes later, two blue-uniformed employees of the Casino would count out and place on the palm of Mister Lucky's hand the amount he had won in the form of crisp new bills, from which Mister Lucky would select one or two, depending on the denomination, and tip the employees. The cocktail waitress would rush to serve him a vodka martini with two olives, as she had been instructed to do when Lucky first started to win the noisy jackpots. She was unfailingly well rewarded.

Mister Lucky became a minor celebrity, and there were usually onlookers watching him play and vicariously joining in his triumphs. It was uncanny too that only he could win jackpots with that particular machine since most people who played the four machines in question, did not last more that an hour without beginning to incur relatively heavy losses. It should be noted that the Mr. Lucky slot in question was the only machine where Mister Lucky could win.

Mister Lucky's Notebook entry for April 15 (which he called the cruelest month inasmuch as he found and lost MM that same month), states that after playing about an hour as always with the machine, he heard sudden popping, saw a flash and smoke, and then she was covered in darkness. The technicians appeared from nowhere and worked on the machine most of the night and Mister Lucky was obliged to retire earlier than usual. Late the next morning, after having a several-course brunch (eggs Florentine, eggs Benedict, grits, smoked salmon, fried catfish, a variety of fruits and juices), he began to play the machine again, but to his dismay, she did not respond. He sensed that she was no longer the same and that her soul had been removed. Lucky rushed to one of the security people asking for an explanation and, in the process became agitated and abusive, was arrested and spent the night in Biloxi Central Lock-Up.

Upon his release Mister Lucky returned to the Casino with a hammer, battering and shattering the machine's glass. Lucky was arrested and taken to Biloxi General Hospital, where he eventually spent a couple of years. Lucky's contention was that the Casino had used and exploited him by setting the machine to pay only when he played and thus attracting more players to the casino who had heard about Lucky's good fortune. He reached a point, while in confinement, when he felt he would not be capable of behaving rationally in the real world, outside the Hospital and, thus he wanted to remain committed. Several unsuccessful suicide attempts were dismissed as Lucky's calculated attempts to remain interned. Unfortunately, with state budget cuts and worsening financial conditions, the authorities decided to release Mister Lucky into the outside world he feared.

Lucky returned to Beau Rivage immediately after his release, and proceeded once more to play his beloved machine. As in the past, Mister Lucky began to win and a small crowd of onlookers gathered around the area. Everything seemed back to normal when suddenly, a flashing light erupted from the machine,

Lucky's body twitched, his hair caught fire and Mister Lucky fell dead. Two eyewitnesses claimed that one of his legs became a goat's hoof as he was being electrocuted. However, the autopsy did not find anything out of the ordinary. Some people who have played the machine since Lucky's death insist that when someone wins a jackpot (which seldom occurs), as Marilyn's voice finishes singing her song and says "tell me you love me true," a faint male voice responds: "I love you true."

Myriads of additional details in Lucky's notebook and in our taped conversations pertain to his life in general, although the vast majority concern expensive menus. Lucky described at great length the food consumed (he became obese during the years he played the machine). These commentaries lack any clinical relevance, as do his ramblings about his sex life (evidently some groupies found it exciting to go to bed with Lucky). Despite the few statements about a male voice heard coming from the machine, no ontological proof exists that it is Lucky's voice.

A West Texas Love Story

Eduardo Guadalupe Romero Martínez was born in Odessa, Texas, April 3, 1954. The city of Odessa is located in the Permian Basin in southwest Texas not far from the border with New Mexico. For all practical purposes, it is a geographic and cultural dessert where the wind blows unremittingly, moaning and whistling under and around closed doors, as the tumbleweeds move about like giant crabs looking for food, and the ubiquitous dust—a dirty-red film that covered everything like a shroud—that gave the town's High School its nickname: "The Red Dust Devils."

Eons ago, sometime during the Paleozoic era, a small inland sea covered the area, its teeming marine life eventually decaying into a sea of oil that transformed the area into an iron orchard of drilling towers and made many of its Anglo citizens very rich. The region has only two towns of any size: Midland, where the oil executives live and Odessa (the armpit of West Texas, some have dubbed it), where the "oil trash," the roustabouts live. Odessa is divided by railroad tracks into North and South, with the Anglos to the north and in the southwest the Mexicans, while the very few African Americans reside in the southeast. During the movement to end segregation, Odessa devised a brilliant solution to the integration problem: designate the Mexicans as white in the south and as minorities in the north, thereby keeping the blacks at bay for many years.

Eduardo Romero Martínez was thus born into an environment less than conducive to becoming anything but a laborer in the fields, maybe a mechanic, or a janitor, as his parents and grandparents before him. But, contrary to the highest expectations and fantasies anyone could have had, he managed under the anglicized name of Eddy Rome to graduate from Yale and then Harvard Law School and become a millionaire by the time he was forty. The story of Ed Rome, Eddy R, to his closest Anglo friends, a fascinating and complicated saga, cannot be told in a straightforward, conventional manner, instead requiring frequent digressions to account for his family background, his "making it," his brilliant career as an attorney, his life in Paris, his three failed marriages (he loved women, but his marriages were riven with quarrels and betrayals), and finally, his return to Odessa (his life an Odyssey minus the mythic dimension), last love and final demise. Edward's life illustrates Oscar Wilde's epigram: "In this world there are only two tragedies. One is not getting what one wants, and the other is getting it."

Eduardo Romero Martínez's life is circular and would best be narrated by concentric recounting circles, taking as the starting point his mother and father: Gloria Martínez Marqués and Guadalupe (Lupe) Romero Heredia. I was Ed's professor of English when he returned to Odessa and decided to seek certification as an English teacher. It is evident that he underwent, as James Joyce would term it, an epiphany in Paris, and decided to return to Odessa and "pay his dues." We met several times a week after he was certified to teach English at Odessa High and had long conversations about his life. When his breast cancer was diagnosed, some two years after he returned to Odessa, our meetings became more frequent and information about his life became more detailed as if he somehow hoped that, by his telling his life-story, he might attain some sort of permanence after his death: he wanted to justify his existence. Ed impressed me as a terribly lonely man. He had become a stranger to his relatives and too "foreign" for Odessa.

Eddie's maternal family was, from the standpoint of the Mexican community, from a good background. Gloria's father (Eddie's grandfather), Bartolomé Martínez Obregón, owned a small grocery store and the family lived in a three-bedroom home on Ada Street. Bartolomé Martínez Obregón claimed to have descended from Spanish immigrants who came to the area in the nineteenth century. His light complexion and green eyes tended to set him apart from most Mexicans in the area. Gloria's mother passed away when she was born so the orphan baby was raised by her aunt, Gertrudis Martínez Obregón, her father's oldest sister. Aunt Gertrudis never married and stayed home helping "Tome" with the store. Gloria resembled her mother: a younger Rita Hayworth with cinnamon skin. While in the eleventh grade at Odessa High School, she had the misfortune of falling into the clutches of the school's principal, Stanley Monahan, at the age of sixteen. Although she was a cheer-leader and very popular, Gloria was a young woman who needed attention since she received very little at home: her father and aunt were very busy at the store. Glo, as some friends called her, helped at the store after school as soon as she learned to add and subtract. As a result, Stan's attention found her vulnerable and one day after school, she lost her virginity in the principal's office. Since Stan was forty, and married, with three daughters, the affair had to be handled very discreetly. He instructed Gloria to take a lot of Home Ec courses, and when she graduated at seventeen, he found her a job at the school cafeteria which facilitated her staying after school ended. This lasted for the better part of a year until Stan's wife, Elsa, became suspicious and, coincidentally, about that same time Gloria missed her monthly "curse," as she called it. In this instance, however, she felt it was better to be cursed than pregnant and she and Stan began discussing their future. She was Catholic enough not to consider an abortion, notwithstanding her committing adultery. Of course, legal abortions would not exist for at least two more decades, and having one was both illegal and dangerous. Gloria had accepted being Stan's lover since she never had enough self-esteem to consider herself worthy of a husband

and a family. On the other hand, the idea of having an Anglo lover, part of a society to which she could never belong, flattered her immature, insecure character. This information was gathered from interviews of friends and acquaintances, newspapers accounts of the subsequent tragedy and some imagination on my part, since Eddie himself was not familiar with all the details included in this narrative. In order to give a complete account of Eddie's tragic life, it seemed essential to include his mother's sad fate which somehow portends Eddie's demise.

Stan and Gloria agreed (she acquiesced to anything he wanted) that she would marry someone not perceptive enough to realize what was going on. Unfortunately, most people had underestimated Guadalupe (Lupe) Romero Heredia all of his life and, in this particular instance that mistake would precipitate tragic consequences. Like an insect attracted to light, Lupe succumbed to Gloria's beauty without questioning the motives of the beautiful woman willing to marry him and consequently was about to be mortally burned. Guadalupe (Lupe) Romero Heredia had been born with a club foot and a slight hunchback (he seemed forever bowing and had trouble looking most people in the eyes). Hence, he could not travel with his father and nine siblings, to do the *pizca* of cotton and other crops, from Lubbock to Wharton and back, year-round. His handicap and related problems at school kept him home, helping his mother from childhood. Eddie always wondered about his father's club foot. There were two literary figures Eddie loved and wished he could meet in the flesh: Brett Ashley and Emma Bovary. From *Madame Bovary* he took the description of Hyppolite's club foot, the better to speculate about his father's. He wondered whether his father's deformed foot was Talipes Equinus, Talipes Varus or Talipes Valgus—did it go downwards, inwards, or outwards? Did his father's deformed foot looked like a horse's hoof? Did he have a pronounced gait? Would there have been a chance that his children (which Eddie would never have), might be affected by such a deformity?

Eddie's father, a very weak child and often ill, quit school in the third grade and stayed home to help with the chores. To make matters worse, childish cruelty knew no end when it came to Lupe's contorted foot. Classmates would snatch his orthopedic shoe and throw it around while poor Lupe limped from one child to another trying desperately to get it back. A circle would form, with Lupe in the center, tottering about to the rhythm of some anarchist composer's tune that only he could hear, as the children passed the shoe around and around chanting, *cojo, cojo, cojo*.

It was Lupe's father, Hector Eduardo Romero Otero, who decided that the child would stay home. With so many children, his mother, Alicia Heredia, needed the help. By the time Lupe was born; the last one of ten, five brothers were over fourteen, and they plus two of the four sisters who were over sixteen, traveled with their father picking crops in the fields of surrounding farms to earn their keep. As the others grew older and work closer to Odessa and within Texas became scarcer, the family traveled farther from home, going to other states with more abundant crops and higher pay. Then Lupe was assigned the task of home-sitting, until he turned sixteen and found work as a janitor at Odessa High School. Two years later, he started working nights, washing dishes at one of Midland's most exclusive restaurants, "Glutece." His life was very Spartan and deposited most of his earnings in a savings account at 3% interest. Except the two or three times a year that his brothers took him to Ciudad Juarez, *para ir de putas*, as his brothers called the visits to the bordellos, he knew no women and seldom went bar-hopping. Lupe was not exactly savvy when it came to women and thus a good target for Stan's schemes.

Lupe had a gift much appreciated by the owner of "Glutece," Clifton Hampton. One evening, as Clifton opened a bottle of Mouton Cadette, 1945, something extraordinary happened. Clifton enjoyed playing host at the restaurant and loved to wear the garb of Sommelier with the chain around his neck dangling the cup used for tasting the wine. This particular evening he was decanting the wine in the kitchen and as he opened it, Lupe, who loved to watch the process, was taken aback by perceiving a strong smell of vinegar and he told Clifton. Clift found it amusing that a Mexican dish-washer could pass judgment of some of his most expensive wine. Upon tasting it, however, he discovered that Lupe had a refined nose, which he decided to put to good use thereafter. Lupe participated in the selection of wines and every bottle's bouquet was subjected to Lupe's discerning nose. As a result, Clifton became very fond of Lupe and decided he would make a picturesque Sommelier: Lupe's rather grotesque figure soon became an added attraction for the restaurant. His garb, the limp, and the tendency to lean forward, reminded many a customer of Quasimodo. Clifton loved to tell the story of the casket of wine and the two wine tasters. One of them declared that the wine had a leathery taste and the other proclaimed that the wine had a rusty, metallic taste. Those around them ridiculed the two tasters until finding, at the bottom of the casket, a key in a leather ring. Clifton felt that Lupe had the potential for being a similarly distinguished wine taster and decided to help him along.

Stan's decision to marry Gloria to Lupe required the intervention of an old friend of his known as *La Mogolla*, the madam of a bordello that Stan frequented until he contracted gonorrhea and decided it was safer to find a mistress. Fortunately his wife, according to Stan, cared little for sex and they seldom engaged in intercourse at all. *La Mogolla*, María Ruiz Torrealba, had been a very attractive, petite woman who amassed a fortune in El Paso during World War II. She moved to Odessa in the late forties when the bordellos multiplied like mushrooms after a rainy night in the El Paso/Juarez area sparking competition too keen for her to continue charging the high prices she once commanded. She arrived in Odessa in her late thirties and, as is usual with prostitutes, was aging fast. La Mogolla decided to open her own "house" and contacted four of the youngest girls she knew in Juarez, opening the only (and therefore best) bordello in Odessa. She was also a "Celestina"—or go-between (the name originates from a famous Spanish literary figure who served as facilitator between lovers, setting up illicit love affairs). *La Mogolla* rented rooms by the hour for those lovers seeking discreet place to meet. Her establishment also offered the only prostitutes in the Permian Basin, with a comparably young and beautiful assemblage. Their youth and beauty earned her bordello the moniker of "the nunnery."

Stan Monahan's closeness to *La Mogolla* made him party to many stories and adventures the young madame had experienced. One particular scam specially fascinated Stan: the sewing of the *labia minores* of young females to simulate virginity. Since female virginity has been so important for many cultures for centuries, ways to have the hymen reconstructed have been invented. A crude way was to use cat's gut to sew part of the inside of the vagina to obstruct the entrance of the penis and to cause some bleeding—enough to stain the "wedding sheets" and allow the groom the satisfaction of having had a virgin. But, not only grooms wanted virgins; the bordellos had clients who requested and would pay high prices for young "virgins," believing that they would escape sexually-transmitted diseases without needing condoms.

They decided that beautiful young Gloria would undergo such an operation before marrying Lupe so that no one would question the girl's honor or purity. Customarily, the groom had the right to return a bride whose virtue was questionable and Stan did not want to take a chance with Lupe—even though he considered the janitor retarded. So glorious Gloria went to visit *La Mogolla* for the necessary "surgical intervention" a week before she married Guadalupe Romero Heredia.

Stan served as the "padrino" and he volunteered, after Gloria had given Lupe her undivided attention during lunch and a few dates that ensued shortly thereafter, with everything initiated by gorgeous Gloria, that he would request Gloria's hand on behalf of Lupe. After all, it would have been very difficult for Lupe to receive permission from Bartolomé Martínez Obregón, Gloria's father, to marry her. Stan, however, with his standing in the community and his wife's fortune (she was old money from ranching before the oil boom), commanded respect. On June 30, 1953, Gloria and Lupe were married in the church of Saint Thomas and many relatives and friends attended the wedding and well-catered reception that followed—thanks to Clifton, the owner of "Glutece."

Stan provided the happy couple with a small house on the South side—his wife owned a large number of the small ranch-style houses that dotted the area where the Mexican Americans lived. They would live rent-free with the understanding that they would do the necessary upkeep and maintenance. Stan took advantage of the opportunity to buy new furniture for his house and gave them some things that weren't too big for the two-bedroom, one bathroom, living-room and kitchen dwelling. He also gave them a 1950 Pontiac which only Gloria drove, taking Lupe to work at the school when they both worked and then at night to his second job in Midland.

This convenient arrangement provided Stan with the means to see Gloria since she would pick him up after taking Lupe to work and smuggle him into the house without the neighbors' noticing. The garage was attached to the house and a door went directly into the kitchen, a very unusual feature for houses on the South Side which, if they had a garage, was detached from the home. The visits of Stanley Monahan continued for several months after the marriage and even when Gloria became visibly pregnant. Informants disagree concerning the number of months she was pregnant upon marriage. Some claim two months, others say only one. I have no way of knowing who was right, nor any idea how these people acquired such knowledge. Some speculated Gloria had a confidant yet to be found. Interestingly, Eddie was born April 2, 1954, nine months exactly after his parents were married so that Stan's paternity becomes questionable. Eddie had expressed to me some uncertainty about which of the two was his biological father (a DNA test was impossible because genetics was in its infancy). Since Gloria was cinnamon-skinned with green eyes, Eddie's resemblance to his mother trumped the question of fatherhood.

The adulterous love affair continued after Eddie was born and Lupe remained unaware that the "padrino" and his wife had a mutual understanding. The house became Lupe's obsession and he started decorating and painting it and remodeled the fireplace which was unusually large for a small house, covering a third of the west living-room wall—until then the only source of heat during the frigid Permian Basin winters. The house acquired central heat only and each room had a small air-conditioner. Lupe loved the fireplace and kept a large supply of wood in his back yard. He bought an axe and, with two of his brothers, would spend a couple of weekends in October hunting for wood. The axe had a red handle and

Lupe kept it sharp enough to cut through the hardest oak as if it were a block of butter.

One day Lupe returned home early. Some say he was informed of the affair his wife had. Others maintain that fate decreed the tragic outcome. Lupe caught them in the act—the beast of two backs—without their knowledge and proceeded to attack them with the axe. The photographs I found with the coroner's report showed Stan and Gloria sliced into several pieces. Some photos revealed numerous abrasions/contusions involving Stan's back, with deep cuts running diagonally from the right shoulder, across the back, to the left flank area. He was beheaded and one of the photos showed the trunk separated from the head. Gloria's corpse photos highlighted the separation of the head and the complete transection of the aorta and pulmonary artery near their origin at the heart, with the heart pierced several times. Since she was under Stan during the attack, she was not as slashed and diced as he.

Lupe, in shock and covered with Stan and Gloria's blood, staggered outside where he was observed by one of his neighbors who called the police. The West Texas media covered the story ad nauseam and I have gathered just about every written report of the incident. A week after avenging his honor, Lupe was found dead in his cell from self-inflicted wounds to the head. Evidently, he committed suicide by ramming his head against the wall, although another rumor had it that he was killed while trying to escape. Baby Eddie was placed in the custody of his grandfather and great-aunt who raised him for a number of years with the aid of Moynahan's widow, who decided to adopt the child and easily convinced his older relatives that Eduardito would have a better future with her. Lacking any explanation for this whim of heiress Elsa Gustafson, I offer several reasons for her fixation on baby Eddie: perhaps she felt obligated to right the wrong committed by his parents; it was a public exhibition of her Christian principles in the "buckle on the Bible Belt;" or perhaps more darkly (the rage of hell was reigning in her heart), to seduce the son of parent(s) who had betrayed and embarrassed her so publicly.

Ed returned to Odessa from Paris, after his divorce from his third wife, Cecile, to do penance for what he felt was a worthless existence and proceeded to obtain certification for teaching English at the secondary level, volunteering to teach at a school located in the South Side, where blacks and Hispanics lived, and for most of whom English was a second language. While completing certification, Eddie began an M.A. in English and wrote a thesis under my direction entitled "Deconstructing the Deconstructors: John Fowles's *Mantissa* and the Parody of Theory."

One of Eddie's favorite novels was *Mantissa* for he considered the novel an onslaught on contemporary theory and its misguided disciples.

When Eddie's cancer appeared, it confirmed his belief that, as he had abused womankind, it constituted an ironically appropriate punishment, given the form of breast cancer. Eddie felt morally and spiritually despicable and believed that not even the disease could extirpate his loathsomeness. The first symptoms of the malignancy appeared as a discharge, suppurating like an infected blackhead, from the left nipple, which he initially rationalized as a blow he received on his left breast while opening the hatchback of his car. After several months had passed, and his white t-shirts continued to display the roundish, red mark of the suppurating left nipple, Eddie decided to consult his internist who immediately assured him that men did not contract breast cancer. Three years had flashed by (as he described his last years in Odessa and on this earth) since Eddie Romero's return to Odessa, and a year from the time his nipple began to discharge blood and pus, when he decided to obtain a second opinion. At this time, a noticeable cyst was growing around his nipple and the second doctor advised a biopsy which came back positive. Eddie's remembrance of the events after the physician said "I am sorry to tell you …," is blurred by the flurry of x-rays, MRI's, exams, nurses, physicians, hospitals, insurance forms, the same questions, telephone conversations that filled the following days and months. He decided that only with the M.D. Anderson Cancer Center in Houston would he be comfortable enough to withstand the torturous treatment awaiting him.

Ed arrived in Houston one Thursday evening in January. It had snowed in Odessa so Houston's weather was pleasant by comparison. He reserved two nights at The Pleasant Inn, a place the Cancer Center recommended, which provided transportation to the Center early in the mornings. Ed saw very few people around and assumed the motel was not doing too well. The following morning, however, he encountered an array of somber, ghostly faces, holding large, yellow manila envelopes where most of their medical history was stored, while riveting their eyes on each other as they wondered what kind of cancer he/she had? Their eyes, Eddie would tell me, with a very dramatic gesture, were the eyes of death! Upon arrival at the M.D. Anderson Cancer Center, he realized again that he was not alone: hundreds of equally curious figures with similarly large envelopes milled aimlessly about, waiting to see their respective physicians, to learn what the treatment would be after surgery: Would it be chemo? For chemo one needed a subclavian "omega port" in the upper chest, below the right shoulder, connected to the subclavian vein so that the very toxic chemicals would go directly into the circulatory system. The injection of those chemicals into the arm would not be practical (they would burn the skin in some cases). Or would it be radiation, with which patients seemed to have returned from some exotic island vacation, but later, the skin peeled-off the area radiated like a banana's, so that even to look at it became painful. Or would the patient have both procedures? Eddie had both: all the hair on his body washed down the drains of Houston and Odessa and his radiated area, like Philoctetes's wound, was an open sore for many months. The substances injected into the "port" included edramoicin, zytoxin, decadron and zofran and the nights and days following the treatment were filled with hallucinations heaved from Dante's Inferno and he sank into the depths of despair.

The only offsetting event during this period in Houston was his meeting Helen Harris, heiress to a cattle fortune from Amarillo, and Ed's last love. She was six years his senior and with her he lived the happiest last two years of his life. Ed met Helen that first morning at the Cancer Center. As soon as he saw her, Eddie said, she intoxicated him with her pastel-blue eyes. The liquor metaphors were felicitous because Ed and I sipped brandy from Jerez and Cognac from France during our weekly chats. Eddie considered himself a connoisseur of life from bottom to top and good liquor was one of his most treasured pleasures. Describing the meeting with Helen, he affirmed that as soon as he was close enough to speak to her, he noticed her ambrosial fragrance. Eddie saw her at a distance, standing against a pillar as the crowd gathered and milled around; their eyes met and she smiled. He approached her not knowing what to say, but as soon as he perceived her scent, Eddie felt he should comment on the fragrance. Helen explained it was a French designer's perfume (the tape was not clear on the name), made exclusively for her, and explained how she participated in the process of selecting and creating the scent. Their treatments coincided, so they saw each other every four weeks and after the affair began, they spent at least a week in New Orleans, in a house in the Quarter owned by Helen. Helen and her husband had had a mutual understanding as to their marriage even before she was diagnosed with breast cancer and, afterward, the breach was more evident and his (Daniel's) resentment of her worsened. Daniel had been a pretty-face dentist that Helen fell in love with after her third husband passed away and she inherited a fortune estimated at $100 million dollars, whereupon Daniel promptly became her fourth husband. A pre-nuptial agreement gave him a monthly allowance and One Million dollars in the event of divorce. About two years into the marriage, she became bored with him—he was no longer fresh and unpredictable, she would say to herself, and Eddie would quote her words to me repeatedly during the last months of his life—when Helen had already crossed over and Eddie was preparing himself to take the giant leap into the unknown. During my weekly meetings with Eddie, I recorded our conversations, allowing me to reproduce some of the most memorable quotes and anecdotes from Eduardo's life.

Eddie Romero's first true love was Elsa Gustafson—the ideal oedipal relationship since there was no father with whom the child had to compete. Elsa was both Eddie's adoptive mother and his tutor (she had a degree in English from Wellesley) until he was fourteen and she then became his lover and mentor on everything she believed a gentleman should be, do, and know. Perhaps this abnormal relationship, as some would judge it, determined Eduardo's behavior during the rest of his life.

Eddie was in Paris studying French in June 1973 when Elsa was hospitalized for a bad fall while tending her roses in the back yard of her mansion; she felt that those roses, that her mother and grandmother had developed through decades to acquire an almost olive green coloration, were hers alone to touch. Eduardo had been staying with a Parisian family that the "Yale Summer in France" program had assigned to him. It had been a long weekend because since that Monday had been a holiday, classes the Friday before were cancelled as well. He had studied French in high school and continue it as a minor at Yale. The fastest manner, he thought, to obtain the hours for the minor was to go with the Yale's Foreign Program in Paris. Furthermore, he was using Paris as a base for his "European experience." That long weekend he had traveled to Helsinki by train with stops en route in Berlin and Copenhagen. Upon his return to the apartment (one of those twilights tinged with red so typical of summer sunsets in Paris, Ed commented), Madame Swifan handed him a telegram from Odessa. There were only four words: "Mother ill/come home." It was signed by Glenda, one of Elsa Gustafson's three daughters.

The following day Eddie was on his way to Odessa arriving on Tuesday and going directly to Odessa General Hospital where Elsa had been taken. He contemplated the most appalling sight his eyes had ever beheld: varicolored wires and disparate tubes connected Elsa to a myriad of machines monitoring and administering medications to her emaciated body to keep it alive. She opened her eyes a minute or two after he arrived and, upon seeing him, whispered "Eduardo." He held her hand for what he felt was too brief a moment hoping to communicate with her, but she seemed to drift into unconsciousness every other second. As he was leaving at the end of visiting hours, the attending physician informed him there was no hope. Because of a fall in her backyard, she was hospitalized, contracting a deadly infection. Ed went home to sleep and the next morning he was awakened by one of the maids with the news that the Señora Elsa had passed away. Eddie felt that the inside of his body leaped outside and became like a sock inside out and, most disturbing, the intense pain burned a hole in his soul. Ed reminisced about Elsa's death frequently, and confessed to me that even so many years after Elsa's passing, he continued to feel the intense pain of the morning the maid came with the message: the remembrance incinerated his soul. He felt like a bull stabbed several times by a clumsy matador. His woebegone expression in the mirror, which Eddy could not help but confront as he shaved that morning, reminded him of the time when his beloved "pantera," a mixed breed dog, was hit by a speeding car. I can imagine the teary olive green eyes that drew women to him. My belief is that Eddie dreaded falling in love because of the difficulty of enduring separation from a loved one.

Eddie went for a long run that morning, circling the outside perimeter of the campus of The University of Texas of the Permian Basin, some two miles in length. He begun running at 9:00 a. m. and was still jogging around at noon, when the temperature was close to 105. Ed told me that his face was covered with perspiration that flowed like a fountain, tears gushed from his eyes, mucous streaming from his nostrils, and that there was a point when he thought his tears had stopped flowing. At that moment, as he run across the "Buffalo Wallow," he saw Elsa crossing the street, waving at him, he waved back as he tripped and fell into unconsciousness.

Ed awoke in the hospital to confront bewildered faces of family and friends gaping at him. The next day, Ed was already in his room at Elsa's Victorian home, still suffering from the loss of his "mother" and wondering about God and the universe. He had read Camus's *The Stranger* his senior year in high school and thought he could react very much like Mersault after hearing about the death of his mother: "Mother died today. Perhaps yesterday." Deficient in his self-awareness, he came to understand by Elsa's untimely death that love was a perilous feeling that one must learn to control. But most importantly, he understood, with the advantage of hindsight, that his suicidal run represented his threnody, his mourning Elsa's death.

Elsa was buried the Saturday after Eddy's return with great fanfare, having been respected by the community for her many generous contributions to the city in particular and the state generally. Ed had very little input into the funeral and was not asked to share his memories of Elsa with those present. He did not mind, Eddie told me one night reminiscing about the funeral, one of the biggest events that year in the Permian Basin, because he realized he would not be able to stammer a word without sobbing out his grief.

The Monday following the funeral he received a note from Glenda, the oldest of Elsa's three daughters requesting a meeting in her mother's office with her sisters, Mary Beth and Lois, and their family attorney. The meeting resulted in a request from the three daughters to take a million dollars and go way quietly (their eyes, according to Ed, were like their father's, a pair of rubber pushbottons). Although Elsa's daughters had moved out of the house when Eddie began living there at the age of seven, he mistakenly thought he was considered a part of the family. Their coldness when indicating that he needed to move on, was very disheartening. In effect, he suffered two blows: the loss of Elsa and the loss of a family.

He moved to Elsa's Victorian home the day of his first communion. She had encouraged Ed's family to take him to mass every Sunday and continued to take him to her church when he began to live in her house. He attended Saint Ignatius, a Jesuit school in Midland, and graduated in the top ten per cent of his class, but with a great deal of assistance from Elsa who tutored him, particularly in the first two years he attended, after which Eddy did it all himself. But Elsa provided him much more than tutoring for school: she taught him the difference between ethics and etiquette; how to please a woman in bed; and with an uncanny awareness of pheromones, Elsa suggested ways of using his perspiration after strenuous exercise, in order to attract the particular female he liked, instead of using synthetic perfumes; how to dress properly preppily; the difference between a Windsor knot and a double knot; how to play a good game of chess; how to prepare and order a good martini (after all, someone named Martinez had concocted it); and a myriad of rules for urbane behavior which he tried to follow his entire life. He also learned from her the joy of reading: if Elsa liked a book, she would spent an entire night finishing it. But, most importantly, Elsa accentuated his having to divest himself of his "brownness," since otherwise it would be very difficult for him to survive in a "white" world. Such was one of the reasons Eddie studied French and never learned standard Spanish.

Interestingly enough, no one reminded Ed of his origins while at school; he wondered whether it was respect or fear of Elsa. But not until the first night she made love to him, did Elsa disclose the tragic death of his parents. From the first day Eddy moved into Elsa's house, when her three daughters had gone to college and eventually married, she considered urgent to erase any vestiges of brownness and suggested anglicizing his name. Elsa commenced Eddie's tutoring as soon as he arrived and that very night showed him how to arrange the table for formal dinners and explained the importance of good manners and civility. Having flown several times a year from the time she was six and her father owned a plane that flew all over the States and Southern Canada, she provided the same education to her three daughters and, around Ed's seventh birthday, he received the same privileges. Edward saw New York and went to a Broadway play by the age of eight, and ate at some of the best restaurants in the United States by the age of fifteen. Eddy lamented often, using a term popular in the seventeenth century, that "marplot cancer" was about to erase all those marvelous memories of his childhood. From Elsa he learned to love one lover at a time and from his uncles he learned to regard women as sex objects. A distant uncle took him once to a bordello in El Paso where Eddy developed an aversion to prostitutes after observing the squalid conditions and later acquired the fear of venereal disease that Elsa instilled in him after she discovered the outing. Feel them, fuck them and forget them was the relative's philosophy which Eddy somehow adopted. Make women happy so that when you whistle, they will run to you, was Elsa's credo. Ed amalgamated both, having one woman at a time and avoiding relationships he knew would not last more than a night. Ed was most women's ideal man with his six-foot frame, a clear complexion and permanent tan, plus olive green eyes which, some women had told him, undressed every female he scrutinized. From the time he was "BMOC" in high school, the quarterback of a mediocre football team, to his first years in Yale, Eddy had numerous short affairs which he ended when he "fell in love" with another beautiful woman.

Ed never provided much detail about his sexual journeys with Elsa, but I was able to ascertain, as he imbibed his French cognac, and the warm liquid traveled from his mouth, teasing his palate, into the esophagus, that a shudder ran through him, and not unlike Proust's madeleine, precipitated his memories of Sunday mornings at Combray. At one point is his late teens Ed believed he was truly the scion of the Gustafson family. After all he had been like a husband to Elsa for most of his teenage years. Elsa's rule was respected at all cost: only when Elsa and Ed were out of town were they to make love. While in the Permian Basin, they were mother and son, rather than man and wife. Eddie was fourteen when Elsa embarked on the most ambitious sex-education project ever devised, preparing Ed to be the lover of women he became. Their age difference caused no problems. In other parts of the world, older women often seduce a young boy and instruct him as to how to please them sexually. Eddy learned about the "G" spot and how to insert his middle finger in the vagina, using the base of the finger to massage the lower portion of the clitoris, called by Elsa, the "Y" spot for "Yes" with exclamation sign. As soon as Elsa exclaimed, "Yes! Yes!," usually a couple of minutes after Eddie began to manipulate her "G Spot" and clitoris, he was to enter hard and quickly, and begin the love-making until orgasm.

In the summer of 1968, at the age of fourteen, Elsa took Eddie to New York and made love for the first time. They ate at "Lutece," a very elegant restaurant, where Eddie put into practice everything he had learned about etiquette: the clothes to wear, which fork to use, dealing with the waiters and busboys, and all relevant information Edward, the urbane fellow, would put to good use the rest of his life. Elsa ordered three courses: the appetizer was crab cakes, followed by a Cesar salad and for the main course duck in order to determine if Ed could manage without using his fingers. The two portions of duck came in deep oval-shaped blue dishes with Chinese characters and a drawing of two flying ducks, resting in a brown sauce and topped with some vegetable unknown to Eddie. Still unsure which of the many utensils to use, he waited for her to show him. Notwithstanding the many home rehearsals he found far more spoons, forks, and knives than on Elsa's table at home. Hence, following her advice to watch his hostess and do exactly as she did, Ed elicited high praise for his performance at dinner. After the felicitous experience in the restaurant, they next attended a Broadway show, *West Side Story*, before returning to the hotel. The room was a suite with a sitting room and the bedroom had two double beds; the bathroom was as luxurious as the ones in Elsa's mansion. He brushed his teeth and got into bed before Elsa did, looking forward to the next day went they would visit the Statue of Liberty and other sites most tourists visited. Elsa went to the bathroom to prepare herself and the room was left in darkness with only neon lights creeping through the window and providing Eddie with a view of a room filled with a kaleidoscope of clashing colors. Ed was extremely surprised to see, at first the shadow and then—reflecting all the colors of the neon signs—Elsa's svelte nude body before his bed. Elsa informed Ed, with the same matter-of-fact attitude with which she taught him many other things, that it was time for Ed to learn about sex. Whereupon, she slipped under the covers, helped Ed remove his pajamas and proceeded to instruct him how to please her sexually. Elsa was in her late forties or early fifties, Ed never knew her real age, and he confessed to me that notwithstanding her age and having had three daughters, her body looked as young as that of his first wife who was in her late teens when he met her. His experience reminded him of the song that describes contemplating the loved one and hearing a hundred gypsies playing violins. Thereafter, he would look at Elsa and love and desire would overwhelm him. He always looked forward to traveling with Elsa and making love to her. During these moments, as he recalled Elsa and spoke to me in a soft monotone, a few subtle tears would escape from Ed's red eyes, glittering with cognac and the myriad of pills he was taking. The chemo had affected his kidneys and liver so that he had to ingest additional medications to keep those organs from deteriorating further.

Edward's first wife was a student of literature at Yale whom he had met while studying French in Paris. Since Ed believed he had to be faithful to Elsa, not until her death did he dare to think about Brett Ashley Oxford as a potential lover. Charismatic, bright, articulate, he possessed the gift of small talk, managing to engage anyone in conversation about anything. He had attended classes in Paris with Brett and they had developed a friendship; when he ran into her at the library the Fall Semester of 1973, they were beginning their sophomore year at Yale. And just as with Helen Harris at the M D Anderson Cancer Center many years later, when he was facing death in the form of breast cancer, what drew Ed to Brett was her scent, not in Paris, but later when he spoke to her in the library, Ed recalled that her hair exuded verbena, which to him was erotic somehow, something voracious and passionate. Brett Ashley was majoring in English and Eddie had taken numerous courses cafeteria style making him very well rounded when it came to the humanities. He had taken all the required courses in math and science, but was unsure what to do about a major. Brett's father was a Professor at Harvard Law School and upon meeting him and developing a friendship, Eddie found in Roger Eastman Oxford, IV the father he never had, his relationship with Brett became formal and he decided to ask her to marry him and become an attorney.

Brett Ashley Oxford had gull-grey eyes (ironic, steely, sparkling eyes that gave her a Mona Lisa look) and red hair (red-auburn as the cognac Ed loved) with a rosy, smooth complexion that reminded him of Elsa and exemplified the female appearance most of Ed's women were to have. Brett's nose recalled Kim Novak and her full lips like Briggite Bardot's, seemed forever pouting and always offering a kiss. Brett Ashley was slim with very long, gymnast's legs, having devoted some of her time to that sport as an adolescent. Brett was five feet, ten inches tall without shoes and when she wore heels she was almost as tall as Ed. After a couple of dates to the movies, and a brief encounter in his apartment, the young people decided to move in together and the affair lasted two years before Ed asked Brett to marry him. A letter from her father assured his acceptance in Harvard Law School, although Ed's GPA was respectable and his LSAT scores were high, the fact that Brett's father was on the faculty assured his acceptance. The marriage was a private one and Eddy's relatives were informed but not invited as he had severed practically all contact with his uncles and aunts. His grandfather and great aunt had already passed away; no one he was close to remained in the Permian Basin, and he had terminated most contacts including school friends.

Upon graduation from Yale in 1975, Eddie entered Harvard Law School and Brett Ashley began graduate work in comparative literature at Harvard. It was an ideal situation: both students at a prestigious institution with a nice income so that financial needs caused no distraction. Two or three years later, shortly before he began clerking at the Chicago Law Firm, Edward realized Brett was having an affair with one of her professors. During those salad days having an "open" marriage was the intellectual thing to do. He discovered Brett's discreet and brief affair when he followed her to the library one night due to suspicions about her demeanor and some dark marks on her thighs that she attributed to hitting herself with the car's door, plus her reluctance to make love as often as they used to. She did not enter the library that night, instead getting into the car of one of her English instructors (one of the professors she was considering to direct her dissertation). Notwithstanding his Hispanic blood, Ed managed to look the other way and continue the marriage until the year he went to clerk for Monroe, Naper & Blakely, a law firm with nine hundred attorneys in offices around the world and a third of them in Chicago were he worked six days per week and fifteen hours per day. That year was like boot camp to Eddie who had managed to escape the Viet Nam War thanks to Elsa's connections and influence. He worked fifteen hours per day and, sometimes, seven days per week. Only five per cent of each class of interns would make partner, and only ten per cent would be hired, so the competition was ruthless and the back-stabbing ubiquitous. Lauren Monroe, (subsequently Edward's second wife), was the granddaughter of one of the founders, George Jefferson Monroe, a partner and director of the mergers and acquisitions division of the firm. She was a very attractive blonde in her fifties, had been married a couple of times and had several affairs with the interns the firm hired every year. Since Ed had had several courses in business and almost enrolled in an MBA program, Corporate Law was dear to him.

As Ed exorcized his demons during our conversation in those unforgettable Permian Basin nights, while sipping cognac and listening to Caruso, verbalizing what had been and what might have been, furtive tears escaped from the corners of his eyes and scrolled down his cheeks. He greatly admired the blind faith of his Catholic relatives who unburdened all their troubles, physical and psychological, onto the *Guadalupana*, or the myriad of saints in the Catholic firmament, accepting stoically their burdens regardless of the outcome: When positive, the Virgin, God, or the saints were to be thanked for the miracle; a negative outcome was the Will of God and his wishes, his design were beyond human understanding. Edward wanted to have enough faith so that the pain caused by the cancer that was devouring him with every passing second would be pacified and he could sleep easily without fear of the unknown, that eternal sleep that was about to descend on him. But it was extremely difficult to evade reality when the skin of his chest looked unnaturally bronzed, where the radiation was killing not only the cancer cells but also the healthy ones, and had a suppurating, foul-smelling wound recalling Philoctetes's wounded foot as punishment for his betrayal. Ed felt he had betrayed womankind and his cancer was just retribution.

As a result of his working long hours in the building of the Law Firm, Ed saw Lauren frequently at all hours. One evening, close to midnight as he was leaving for his apartment, as the two of them were in the elevator, she asked him if he would like to have a drink with her. She was interested in knowing the opinions the interns had of the firm and that was an opportunity to do so. They chose a tavern about two blocks from the building called "Rick's Place." The decor was a homage to Humphrey Bogart's films, *Casablanca* in particular, with walls plastered over by Bogie's posters, piped-in music from Bogart's films, and attendants in Arab costumes. Several isolated enclosures, fitted with curtains shaped like Bedouin tents, invited those customers who desired privacy and Lauren requested one that particular night. As the maître d', dressed in a black tuxedo led them to their booth, "As Time Goes By" was playing. The booth contained lots of memorabilia from *Casablanca,* with posters and quotes from the film, in large bold letters, scattered throughout the booth: "The Germans wore gray, you wore blue;" "Tell me, who was it you left me for? Was it Laszlo, or were there others in between? Or—aren't you the kind that tells?" "Kiss me. Kiss me as if it were the last time;" "Round up the usual suspects;" "We'll always have Paris." The last quote was particularly ironic in view of Ed's residence in Paris and his eventual marriage to a Parisian. The private enclosure held a small table with two chairs across from each other and, as they sat, their feet touched. Lauren did not stir. Eddy felt a tsunami of emotions overtaking his body. Later, as they sipped martinis, and chatting about the firm, she removed her shoes, placing her right foot on Ed's lap. Whereupon he massaged her black-stockinged foot while placing it on the erection he had had since arriving at the tavern. They left Rick's place and went to Ed's apartment where they made love, repeating these evenings often thereafter. Eddie told me, remembering that night and quoting another of Bogart's film, that notwithstanding their conversation, which had concerned mostly business, his plans for the future and other interns (since she was interested in obtaining the best of them for the firm), was for him a romantic experience because of the music: "You can say much more with a few bars of music than a basketful of words." Ed feared that his life, all he had observed and experienced, risked disappearing like tears in the rain, so I became his confidant and thus his amanuensis.

Edward was hired by Monroe, Naper & Blakely a year later and shortly thereafter divorced Brett Ashley. He became a star in the firm and in two years he rose to partner and married Lauren. Those were his salad days, hobnobbing with the high society of Chicago, married to one of the most powerful women in the city and wealthy beyond belief. Very few could say he did not have the credentials since his degrees from Yale and Harvard were invaluable and his work ethic earned millions for the firm in two short years. He was a genius when it came to mergers and acquisitions and, naturally, a despicable bastard to some but a hero to those he provided the leverage to attain immeasurable riches. Ed was ruthless when it came to design the necessary maneuvers to secure the expected results, caring nothing, about widows or orphans and pensions for old men who constituted obstacles to desired harvests. He became a notorious corporate raider.

The Law Firm had a small office in Paris which Ed and Lauren visited during a month of honeymooning in Europe. They decided then that Edward should spend a couple of years developing the firm's interests there by hiring for expansion in the economic environment that the European Union would soon provide. Edward would travel to Chicago and spend long weekends with Lauren and managed, thanks to his hard work and business virtuosity, to turn the Paris Office into one of the most productive of Monroe, Naper & Blakely. However, the living arrangement took a toll on Eddy's marriage and after some ten years it ended abruptly.

Following the collapse of his third marriage with a French woman, Cecile Parrottin, some three years afterwards—half his age chronologically, but much more sophisticated and mature than he—Eddie returned to Odessa in the early nineties after what he called his "long journey into night": For several weeks after Cecile left him, he drank himself into a stupor with absinthe and pastis, forcing himself to vomit copiously. He described the nausea and vomiting as an exorcism to expel his demons. He would go to the "Café Mably" on Boulevard de la Redoute, or two of his favorites in the Beauvoisis district: "Café des Bretons" and the "Bar de la Marine," order his drinks and listen to the music these establishments provided their patrons. It was usually jazz featuring numerous black female singers. One of his favorite songs was the one that had the following verses: *One of these days, you'll miss me honey*, and he would sink into the depths of despair, guilt, and self-pity, progressively deeper as he downed the combination of absinthe and pastis (gulping a glass of each in turn, seldom reaching eight), and by the time eleven came around, he had already vomited a pair of demons and his clothes and breath exuded a foul stench. Thanks to his large tips and his being a discreet drunk, he was never barred from any of the cafes. One evening while vomiting in the men's room of "Café Mably," imagining his insides about to erupt from his mouth and remembering his second wife whom he had betrayed so ignominiously, he experienced a vision of himself in Odessa helping other Mexican Americans.

Cecile had been the result of his mid-life crisis and prolonged stays away from Lauren, the typical man of a certain age falling in love with a woman much younger than he. While living in Paris he was asked to teach a class on Corporate Law at the Sorbonne. The first day of classes she was sitting on the front row of a large auditorium and, upon seeing her, Eduardo told me, he immediately recalled, like a teenager in love, Romeo's words: "What light through yonder window breaks?" He perceived a halo around Cecile's head and was immediately intoxicated with her looks: Very short red hair, rosy flesh and green eyes that seemed to question, ironically, every word Ed said in his halting French. One week into the semester they had their first date and, soon thereafter, a passionate affair began. As a Francophile, Ed believed that French was the ideal language for foreplay and bedroom chatting. He loved it when Cecile whispered in his ear dirty sweet nothings. Cecile's wealthy parents did not object to her having an affair and eventually marrying Ed. Edward, having heard rumors of his wife's affair with a new intern and seeing each other so seldom after a few years of marriage, fortified his rationalization for the affair and the eventual divorce. To Ed's distress, Cecile absconded from their penthouse taking only the golden toothbrush handle he had bought her for her birthday at Tiffany's. It had several precious stones encrusted and he obsessively recalled how the stones reflected the sun-light coming through the window as he watched his White Goddess's nude body, with a derrier that was a sodomist's dream, her beauty blinding him, so many mornings in Paris, while she brushed her teeth. The rest of his gifts, all her clothes, shoes, jewelry, everything remained. If Cecile had not left him a note, he would have wondered if something terrible had happened. Her note was brief and cold: "Ed, I am moving in with a girl friend. Adieu." Simone was an old friend of hers and a rather homely woman, according to Ed, who saw her socially and never imagined that Cecile could have such terrible taste as to leave him for such an individual. He felt that if Simone had been a man he had ways to deal with it. If there was anything sexual between Simone and Cecile, he had no idea as to how to win Cecile back.

The last three weeks of Eddie's life depressed me enormously. Our final nights together, although we met more often, were limited to my staying a few minutes while he rested on his bed and naturally we spoke little as he was so emaciated from the cancer that overwhelmed his body, making his face and body a grotesque parody of the muscular, handsome Edward. His permanently tan complexion had turned chalky, his beautiful eyes were sunken and had lost their sparkle: It seemed like looking into muddy waters down a dark well. Wealth allowed him to hire several nurses around the clock at home. My visits were moments of joy for him, but he was too medicated to sustain a conversation for very long. At times he would sing or mumble old songs from the Catholic mass ("He will raise me up on the last day …") which seemed to give him peace. The last week of his life, after I informed him that Helen Harris had passed on (they had stopped seeing each other several months earlier), he asked for a priest. I immediately contacted Saint Catherine and Father John, I believe the priest's name was, visited him and Ed received communion. A few days later, one of the nurses called, informing me that Ed had expired in his sleep.

I think my nightly conversations, our *tête-à-têtes,* provided the best moments in my life, for he had lived well if not very long. I could never have afforded to visit all the places in the planet Ed visited, or to enjoy his business experience and women, but vicariously savored those unattainable pleasures. I have lived my entire life in West Texas and am an Ab.D. finishing my Ph.D. from Texas Tech University which unfortunately, has taken longer than usual due to duties at my present position at the University of Texas of the Permian Basin. Other than attending professional meetings in different cities in the United States, I've never enjoyed the pleasure of traveling abroad. It seemed my duty to provide the world with Edward's insights into life as well as what I learned while listening to him so many nights in Odessa. Ed was truly insecure with a pathological need for approval and repeatedly wished and hoped that after his death, he would be remembered often, with kindness. Hopefully, the present text may fulfill Eddy R's last wish.

www.ingramcontent.com/pod-product-compliance
Ingram Content Group UK Ltd.
Pitfield, Milton Keynes, MK11 3LW, UK
UKHW041839200726
13854UKWH00003BA/1216

9 780595 421046